A CHILLING RECEPTION

WHEN A WEDDING TURNS DEADLY

PIPPA FINN MYSTERIES
BOOK TEN

POPPY BLYTHE

PUREREAD.COM

CONTENTS

DEAR READER, GET READY FOR ANOTHER GREAT COZY...

READY TO SOLVE THE MYSTERY?

Pippa is delighted as Callie and Tim finally get to tie the knot! It's a beautiful ceremony at the church, and the clumsy handyman manages to make it through the entire day without causing an accident.

Unfortunately, their wedding doesn't remain uneventful. The reception is being held at a hotel. Pippa discovers one of the staff members has died, and it looks like poison. Who is to blame; another member of staff, or one of the guests?

Turn the page and let's begin

∽

1

Love and God's grace was in the air. The day was one of those that seemed to rush by far too quickly yet at the same time last forever, and if any day was to be the one that defined the rest of eternity then it should have been this one, Pippa thought to herself. It was a most anticipated day, the union of love between Tim and Callie in holy matrimony. Despite not being the bride, Pippa had felt her fair share of nerves as she was the maid of honor. Thankfully the wedding had not had too many dramas. The main one had been when Tim's family had booked out most of the hotel rooms. Pippa had been forced to turn her attention to navigating the social minefield while making sure that Callie was as relaxed as possible. Weddings, while joyful, could also bring about a lot of stress, and Pippa merely wanted the day to go splendidly for Callie.

Pippa and Jack had devoted themselves to making sure that the happy couple had the happiest day. They watched Tim as he went about his life, making certain that he would not get into any mishaps before the wedding. There had been a few heart-stopping moments, but by and large he was fine.

Callie had been getting more and more nervous as the days went by. At first she had been excited and composed, but the anxiety flooded through her and she paced around the floor of her café, conjuring up myriad reasons why she could not go through with the wedding. Whenever this happened Pippa would put on a cup of tea, because everyone knew that a warm cup of tea solved everything, and ask her if she loved Tim and if she thought that Tim could make her happy. Callie replied in the affirmative, and Pippa told her that as long as she kept asking herself these questions and as long as the answers remained positive then she did not have anything to worry about.

Pippa's heart swelled with joy for the happy couple. Her life had been filled with examples of failed romances. It was enough to make anyone jaded and bitter, and that's not to mention the grisly examples of betrayal she had seen while helping investigate various murders. So to see two people find happiness in this often cruel and dark world was a reminder that God blessed those with a pure heart, and he would help guide soul mates together.

Just, as she thought, he had done so for her and Jack. A smile drifted across her face and for a moment she felt herself slipping into a wonderful world of dreams as she thought about Jack's handsome face and his charming smile and the general sense of warmth he exuded. He was indeed a special man, and she felt blessed to be able to call him a friend... and more. Over the past few months she and Jack had become close, slipping into a relationship, almost. It was surreptitious, wrapping around her like the first sign of a summer's breeze. It was two hands brushing against each other while out walking Jasper, laughter shared while cooking a meal, resting her head on his shoulder as she fell asleep while watching a film, a gentle kiss shared under the stars and the moon, as though the heavens themselves were blessing their union. A part of Pippa was still unsure where this was going or what was happening. A whirlwind of emotion could take hold of her mind, but with him the moments were always quiet and she realized that she did not need to think about the future so much. It was enough to just be with him and enjoy the moments.

But, of course, the present day was not about him. They had seen each other in the morning. He had prepared breakfast for her and looked after Jasper while she went to help Callie get ready. Callie had her hair styled in a way that Pippa had never seen her wear before, and it was very fetching. She looked beautiful, as did all people who were in love. Callie's cheeks blushed at the compliment and she expressed a wish that everything should go well during the day. Pippa promised it would.

She helped Callie get into her elegant, white wedding dress. While tying together the lace around Callie's back, Callie turned and looked over her shoulder.

"Do you think you'll be wearing one of these soon?" Callie asked.

"I don't think so," Pippa said, laughing nervously.

"But I thought things were going well between you and Jack?"

"They are, but it's still too early. We're just enjoying being with each other. There's no need to rush into these things. Besides, with his history I don't even know if he'd want to get married."

Pippa's voice caught on emotion as she said this. Before she had arrived in Burlybottom on Sea she hadn't thought of herself as the kind of woman to get married. She had always been a forward thinking, modern woman who saw marriage as an archaic tradition that only existed to control women. However, the more time she spent with Callie and saw how the engaged couple interacted with each other the more Pippa realized that she had allowed herself to be swayed by the rhetoric of the cynical. Indeed, marriage had been used as a business transaction in the past, and in some cases in the modern world that was still true, but at its best it was a choice between two people to put their trust and faith in each other, and to center everything around the Lord leaping into the unknown holding hands and promising to be there for each other no matter what. Was there any greater display of faith in the world?

Pippa was not sure, and the more she thought about it the more she realized that she would like this for herself. But she was not the only one who had to make the decision, and she had not broached the subject with Jack yet. She knew how much the past still affected him, how the savage dagger of pain twisted in his heart. There was a woman who had walked this path before her, who had died before they could speak the sacred vows. Could Pippa take Emily's place? She hadn't asked because she was afraid of the answer, and so for now she was content in basking in the comfortable glow of what they shared. But, in the back of her mind, there was always the possibility...

She did not want something like this to distract her from her task though, and so she focused her attention back on Callie. She arranged Callie's hair piece and once the bride was ready, Pippa got dressed herself. She was wearing a muted blue gown that flowed along her body and billowed out toward the ankles, a little like a mermaid's tale. She wore corn flour blue flowers in her hair, which was tied up in an elegant ponytail and swung between her shoulders like a pendulum.

Jack had called in a favor with someone he knew, and so at the top of the hour the sound of hooves clopping against the main street of Burlybottom on Sea could be heard. Pippa looked outside to see a carriage being drawn by two powerful steeds. The driver waited for Callie and Pippa to step out of the house and then helped the two women up into the carriage. She and Callie settled in the plush leather seats and giggled with each other as they looked out toward the horizon, gazing into forever. Pippa wondered if Callie was seeing a life with Tim, a life filled with love and children that would spill all over Burlybottom on Sea, spreading joy and happiness to anyone who encountered them. Then, Pippa thought about her own future. She averted her gaze and swung her head low so that Callie would not see the redness upon Pippa's cheeks. Was she the type of person to want a family? Back in London she would have scoffed at such a thought. She and Clive were a modern couple, concerned with increasing their financial portfolio and amassing a great deal of property and wealth. Children had been the last thing on their minds because they had been busy and occupied with so many other things, but things were different in Burlybottom on Sea...

"It's so beautiful, isn't it? I can't believe this is actually happening to me. I thought I was going to have to leave this place to find my happy ending," Callie said. Her voice trembled and Pippa realized that Callie was close to tears.

"You can't cry yet. You'll ruin your makeup!" Pippa exclaimed. Callie laughed. "I think that when you're a good person happy endings have a way of finding you. God makes sure of it."

"So what's your happy ending going to be Pippa?" Callie asked, wiping her eyes with a single slender finger and composing herself. Pippa found herself staring into space because she could not think of an answer. The horses whinnied, as if they were trying to give her a hint, but Pippa remained mute.

They arrived at the church. Jack was waiting in the doorway with Jasper by his side. The dog's tail was wagging and his tongue was hanging out. He might not have been able to understand the significance of the day, but he knew that something exciting was happening. Jack looked even more handsome than ever. He wore a smart suit that was perfectly fitted to his strong body. His hair, which was usually tousled from working in the fields all day, was slicked back. Pippa thought he looked like a movie star, as though he had just leapt off the screen to dazzle her. The driver helped the ladies down, and Jack approached them.

"Tim is waiting for you inside. He stumbled up the stairs, but thankfully he hasn't done anything clumsy," Jack said, holding his arm out for the bride. Callie took it. Pippa and he shared a loving smile. She bent down and petted Jasper quickly, who fell into step with Pippa and entered the church.

The church was filled with all the residents of Burlybottom on Sea, as well as members of Tim's family. Callie had been quite self-conscious about the fact that she did not have a family to call her own, and was afraid that she would feel like a guest at her own wedding. However, Pippa reminded her that everyone she knew in Burlybottom on Sea was her family. They had proven that time and time again, and on this day it was clear that Callie was loved. Everyone turned to see her and there was an audible gasp at the sight of the beautiful bride. Whispers were shared, and she outshone even the vivid display of color created by the dresses and flowery hats on display.

Rich music filled the air as Jack led Callie down the aisle. Pippa noticed Arthur and his wife, smiling at them happily. She watched the ceremony unfold, holding her bouquet of flowers tightly. Tim was shaking with nerves, although Callie's presence helped settle them. The Reverend gave a lovely reading and the hymns they sung referred to the glory and the majesty of God's love. It was eternal and perennial and enduring, just as the love between Callie and Tim would be. Pippa found her gaze drifting toward Jack, picturing herself standing up there with him and speaking the vows herself. It wasn't something she ever used to imagine herself doing, but it was a sign of how much she had changed since arriving in Burlybottom on Sea, as though she had emerged from a chrysalis, now fully formed.

There was only one moment of potential drama, when Tim took the ring from his best man, he almost fumbled it. The ring bounced from one hand to the other and there was another audible gasp rising from the guests, this time more from fright than of awe. Somehow Tim always managed to get himself into a little bit of trouble, and Pippa did not know how Callie was going to cope with things for the rest of her life. But instead of the ring bouncing on the floor and rolling back down the aisle, Tim managed to pluck it out of the air in a curled fist. He breathed a sigh of relief and smiled. There was a ripple of applause, and then the ceremony continued with the couple sealing their vows and becoming more committed than they had been before.

Pippa didn't realize she was crying at first. It was only when she felt the warm trickle flowing down her cheeks that she became aware. She felt silly for letting these emotions get the better of her, but if it was going to happen then it might as well have been at a wedding. The world was filled with misery and grief, so on days like these when the beacon of God's grace shone upon the world it was important to take stock and fully appreciate it, because these were the kind of days that were worth living. These were the kind of days that showed the true meaning of life.

2

"You're looking very handsome today," Pippa said as she greeted Jack with a kiss on the cheek.

"And you're looking lovely. Would it be rude of me to say that you're even more beautiful than the bride?" he asked with a twinkle in his eye. It brought a smile to Pippa's face.

"I suppose it would if you told the bride that, but as long as we keep it between ourselves I think it will be fine."

She linked her arm in with Jack's and took part in the photos when she was called for. It was a perfect day, with the sun shining upon the chapel and making it glow as though it had been painted by a master artist. The grass was a vivid green, the sky azure blue, and it did not seem that there could be anything going wrong with the world.

The wedding party soon moved away from the church though. Because of the number of Tim's family in attendance they had booked the reception to be in a posh hotel on the outskirts of the town, in fact the same hotel that Pippa had been too before when chasing a suspect on her last case. She certainly hoped that her visit this time would be less eventful. A parade of cars traveled toward the hotel, which also boasted a spa and a golf course, catering to people who liked to escape from their hectic lives for a while. Pippa couldn't help but wonder how much it cost, and thought that Tim's business must have been doing well.

The food was delicious; she had a cut of roasted beef with crispy roast potatoes and crunchy vegetables. She was sitting at the head table between Jack and Callie, while Tim's entourage stretched out at his end. At the table nearest her were Braw Ben, Arthur and Sophie, and a few people she did not recognize. The conversation was lovely and Braw Ben seemed to be in his element. His loud voice reaching Pippa's ears, telling all kinds of stories about other weddings that had taken place through the years, although as with every story Braw Ben told, it had to be taken with a grain of salt. Another table housed Pippa's former neighbors, whose lilting voices carried across to her as they dominated the conversation at their table. The room was filled with the tinkling of cutlery and the warm laughter of people having a merry time. The guests were only silent when it came time for the speeches. Tim was clearly nervous, and ended up dropping his sheets of paper which became disorganized, but eventually he managed to get everything settled and gave, a somewhat surprisingly, moving and poetic speech.

"I didn't know the chap had it in him, good on him" Arthur said. Congratulations and cheer were passed on from all the crowd and best wishes were given to the happy couple. There were some more photographs taken, and Pippa was featured in many of them given her position as maid of honor, and thankfully there did not seem to be anything that demanded her attention. The day had gone smoothly, which was more than any of them could have asked for.

As the evening moved on, the party began and music filtered through the room. People were buoyed by the fine, happy mood of the day and were eager to embrace the delight that now came easily to them. Callie and Tim had provided disposable cameras on every table so that guests could take pictures of themselves, which would provide a greater scope of the day than what a single photographer could muster, especially because he was mostly concerned with the married couple. The clicking and whirring of these cameras was a constant sound as Pippa moved around the room. As the maid of honor, it was her duty to try and meet as many people as possible. She tried to speak to everyone briefly, and checked to make sure that there weren't any problems. Most people had a rosy glow about them and their eyes were filled with happiness.

She came to Braw Ben, who was sitting in his chair, gazing out at the sight of people dancing before him.

"Are you okay Ben?" she asked.

Ben smiled, a hazy look in his eyes. "Oh I'm fine, just fine Pippa. Isn't it a fine day? It's been too long since we've enjoyed something like this."

"I agree, although I was worried you might feel a little put out that they didn't choose to have the reception at your pub."

Braw Ben laughed heartily. "You think I'm going to complain about a day off Pippa? Perhaps you don't know me as well as you thought," he leaned forward, his words riding the fading laugh. "I wouldn't be able to put on a spread as good as this, and my pub isn't big enough either. Besides, it's nice to be able to get to put my feet up for once and relax. The thing about hosting a party is that people forget the host never has a good time because they're always too concerned about everyone else enjoying themselves. I'm thankful for the break. But that reminds me, the next time you come to the pub you need to ask me what I have for you. You haven't come to see me about that surprise yet."

Pippa thought back and remembered that indeed Jack had mentioned that Braw Ben had said that he had a surprise in store for her when she returned from Leeds. That had been a good while ago now, but it had slipped her mind.

"I'm sorry Ben, it must have gotten away from me. There has been so much going on."

"I know Pippa, there's no need to apologize. Besides, I think it's the kind of thing you're only going to want when you're ready, but something tells me you're ready now."

He wore a cryptic smile, while Pippa gave him a puzzled look. She was about to ask Ben what he meant when she noticed someone coming up behind him. It was Jack. She knew it before she even saw his face, because she had become attuned to his presence. He touched the inside of her elbow and she turned around.

"Do you mind if I steal you for a few moments? I was hoping to dance with the maid of honor," Jack said.

"I think that can be arranged," Pippa smiled, and then looked a little regretful. "I'm sorry that I've been wandering around the room. I haven't intended to ignore you."

Jack shook his head, indicating that he understood. He led her to the dance floor as the music changed from a high tempo song to something slower and more romantic. Pippa glanced at his feet. "Where's Jasper?" she asked.

"Jasper is quite fine," Jack said, nodding to the far side of the room. Pippa peered through the throng of dancers and saw Jasper following a white dog. They went back and forth and played with each other. It seemed as though romance was touching all the souls in the hotel, not just the human ones. Pippa chuckled to herself and then wrapped her arms around Jack's neck, as his hands fell to the small of her back. They swayed to the rhythm of the music. She let herself fall into his easy presence, placing her head against his chest, enjoying the steady thrum of his heart. It was an unwavering beat, something that she could anchor herself to even in the stormiest seas, and something she could count on even when the world itself seemed as though it was crumbling apart.

"You know, I was just thinking about how you've always been there for me ever since I arrived in Burlybottom on Sea," she murmured.

"And I remember how you came to the farm looking as though you wanted to be anywhere else."

Pippa laughed. "I didn't realize then how special this place was, or how much treasure was hidden here."

"Well, the treasure wasn't technically here…"

"I wasn't talking about that kind of treasure. I was talking about the treasure that can make people's lives better. I'm talking about you Jack I just… you mean so much to me. I'm not sure that I can ever put into words exactly how much."

"I feel the same Pippa," he said in a deep voice that rolled over her like thunder and left her just as shocked.

"You do?" Pippa tilted her head up to look at him directly.

Jack smiled and nodded his head ever so slightly. "Of course I do Pippa. Is it really in doubt?"

"Well... it's just that with how you felt about Emily..."

Jack's expression turned serious. "I know that my past has been a sensitive subject for me, but for a long time I felt myself rooted to the past. You helped me sever those roots and move forward. You reminded me that I am capable of loving again. As soon as I met you I realized that you were not like anyone I had ever known before. And the more I got to know you the more I came to be impressed by your spirit, your passion and your strength. You are a remarkable woman Pippa, and do you really think I would abandon my farm and drive up to Leeds for just anyone?"

"I don't suppose you would," Pippa said, a wide smile spreading over her face. Jack cocked an eyebrow and their heads bowed toward each other, drawn taut by the strings of love.

The song ended soon after this and the DJ announced that it was time to cut the cake. Pippa was so lost in her own happiness that she almost forgot the danger of Tim being left alone with a long, sharp knife. She dragged Jack to the small stand where the three tiered cake was, and watched, wincing as Tim took the knife in his hands. Someone then called out his name to be careful and as he turned his body to try and see who had said this, he bumped the table and the cake teetered. People held their breath as they feared the cake would topple over, but it just barely managed to remain upright. Another disaster had been averted. God was certainly watching over them today.

Callie then took the knife from Tim and stood in front of him, making sure that he was as far from the table as was possible while still being able to put his hands upon hers and guided the knife through the cake. There was a loud cheer as the icing was split and crumbs of the cake began spilling out. Pippa helped serve the cake, but it was so big that there was plenty left. Callie mentioned that she did not know where to store it, so Pippa said that she would find the hotel representative who was taking care of the wedding party to find out.

This representative was a kindly woman, by the name of Jessica. She was around Pippa's age and had been a good servant to the married couple, answering any questions they had and making sure that the hotel was properly prepared for them. Pippa walked out of the hall and was immediately struck by how different the atmosphere was outside. The raucous noise from the party barely bled out through the walls, and the rest of the hotel was carrying on as though nothing special was happening at all.

Pippa peered along hallways, but could not see anyone there. She then went to the reception desk, but that was empty as well. She pressed a bell for attention, but when nobody appeared for a couple of minutes she decided to continue her investigation. Ever since they had arrived at the hotel Jessica had made herself available for the wedding party, so it seemed strange that she would just disappear without a word. Pippa checked outside, just in case Jessica had stepped out for some fresh air, but she was nowhere to be seen there either. If she had gone on a break then perhaps there was a staff room. As Pippa returned toward the main hall she noticed that the hallway tapered off, and there was a room labeled as 'staff only'. Pippa shrugged and rapped her knuckles on the door. There was no response, but the door was not completely closed, and creaked open.

Pippa took this as an invitation and stepped into a shadowed room. Since it was dark she didn't think that anyone would be inside, but as light shone into the room she noticed that someone was sitting there, directly in the middle of the room.

"Hello? Jessica?" Pippa asked. It certainly seemed like Jessica's hair, but she had her back to Pippa. Her nose twitched at a rancid smell, but she tried to ignore this for the time being. "I don't mean to intrude, it's just that we were hoping you might be able to help store the cake for a while. It's been cut and there's plenty left. I'm sure that you can help yourself to a piece if you like. You've certainly earned it," Pippa continued speaking as she went into the room. She hoped she wasn't causing offence, as she knew that sometimes hospitality workers could put so much of their energy into being friendly while working that on a break they needed time to recharge. However, still Jessica was not replying, and Pippa's instinct told her that something was very wrong.

When she reached out and touched Jessica's shoulder, Jessica's head lolled back and lifeless eyes stared at Pippa. Pippa leaped back in shock, retracting her hand immediately. She gasped and then her heart sank.

Callie and Tim's perfect day had been marred by murder.

3

Although Pippa did not want to leave the body alone, she couldn't stay in the room with it. She took a few moments to quickly inspect the body. There weren't any visible marks like stab wounds, but the lips were dark and vomit was drying on Jessica's chin and clothes. Given the fact that Jessica hadn't displayed any sign of being unwell, it seemed as though she had been poisoned. And if it was something to do with the food, then the guests might be in danger as well.

She took a breath and left the room, this time pulling the door closed behind her and striding back to the main hall. She surreptitiously got the attention of Jack and Arthur.

"Do you know if anyone has been complaining of feeling ill? Or have you seen anyone rushing to the bathroom?" Pippa asked.

Arthur and Jack looked at each other and frowned, shaking their heads. Pippa breathed a sigh of relief.

"Okay, at least that means it might not be widespread," she said.

"What might not be widespread?" Arthur asked.

Pippa puffed out her cheeks and lowered her voice, making sure that nobody else would hear what she had to say. "I think that Jessica has been murdered."

Jack gasped and Arthur was all business. He excused himself for a moment as he had to tell Sophie. She accepted the news with equanimity. It must have been difficult for her, Pippa thought, for no matter where they went there might always be a call to action for Arthur. As soon as this was settled Pippa took them back to the room, this time turning on the light properly. Jessica's eyes were hollow and gaunt. Her skin had a sickly shade to it. Arthur got as close to the body as he could without touching it.

"I did see her earlier. She certainly seemed in good spirits," Arthur said.

"But there have been cases where people have died of no good reason before, right?" Jack asked.

"Indeed, but given her age it's highly unlikely. Poison would explain the shade of her skin, and the vomit," Arthur replied.

"I couldn't see any marks on her body that would indicate a stabbing or some other violent attack either," Pippa said. They began to move around the room, looking for clues, but there wasn't anything that stuck out to them. "What are we going to do about this? I mean, I know that we need to find a killer, but Callie and Tim are also having such a good day so far and the last thing I want to do is disrupt that."

"I can make sure that nobody finds out this has happened," Jack said.

Arthur looked troubled. Pippa knew that his oath to pursuing justice was going to be at odds with his desire to protect Callie and Tim for forever thinking about murder when they looked back on their own special day. His brow was knotted as he considered the matter, and then he spoke in that brusque, authoritative way he had. Despite their pleasant working relationship, Arthur was always the constable and Pippa would follow his orders, even if she disagreed with them.

"Keep an eye on people. Try to make sure that nobody leaves," Arthur said.

"You think one of the guests could have done this?" Jack asked, gaping toward Arthur.

"I think at the moment, we can't afford to rule anyone out. But you're right, until there's a reason to do so we should let Callie and Tim enjoy their wedding day. We should speak to the staff first. Perhaps one of them knows something. We might discover that we don't need to tell anyone else at all."

The trio exchanged a somber look before they left the room. Jack held the door open for Pippa. As she walked out she looked down the corridor toward the angled corner and noticed a bell boy staring at her. His face was the picture of shock. He froze for a moment, but then regained his senses and rushed away.

"I wish I hadn't left Jasper in the hall," Pippa lamented.

"We don't need Jasper," Jack muttered as he blistered past Pippa, his legs pumping as he ran in pursuit of the bell boy. Pippa and Arthur gave chase behind him. Pippa liked to keep fit and was usually quite athletic, but in this instance she was wearing heels and so found it difficult to keep her balance. Arthur, who was a few decades older, did not have the same stamina as he used to. And, as he put it, he was fond of the luxuries in life. He liked to proclaim that discipline and an ascetic lifestyle was the respite of the young, for they had the time to abstain from things.

They followed the corridor around. Jack cornered the bell boy near the reception area. Jack had caught him and pressed the boy against the wall. He was thin, in his late teens. His golden name badge read 'Gavin'.

"Please don't hurt me. Please," Gavin bemoaned, the words tumbling from his mouth as readily as the tears flowed from his eyes. He shook his head vehemently and as soon as Jack realized how distressed the boy was, he released his grip and stepped back. Gavin put his hands up and shook his head from side to side, trying to fight off whatever he thought was going to happen to him. "Please, I didn't mean to do anything."

Pippa's ears pricked up. She stepped forward, ready with a sharp question that would cut to the heart of the matter. Was Gavin referring to the murder, was there some other misdemeanor he had committed, or was he simply referring to the fact he had been spying on them? However, before she could ask this question she was interrupted by the sudden appearance of a tall, brooding man with broad shoulders. He emerged from the door behind the reception desk with a stern look on his face. He wore a jacket and a crisp shirt, with cufflinks that gleamed as they caught the light. He had a round face. His hair was shaved short. He had a goatee as well, and his eyes were piercing. His voice was commanding, and it was clear to Pippa that he was the manager. Like Gavin, he wore a gold name badge. His name was Frank.

"What's going on here? Why is my employee being manhandled? Get away from him immediately," Frank said, glaring at Jack. He must have thought they were rowdy guests who had let alcohol get the better of them. Pippa thought it must have been a risk for those in the hotel trade to make themselves vulnerable to dealing with unpredictable and rash people. Frank beckoned Gavin with one jerk of his hand, and Gavin peeled himself away from the wall. Pippa watched the boy and could not tell if he was relieved or afraid. He bowed his head and went to stand beside Frank, using his manager as a shield.

"My name is Arthur Bell and I'm a police officer, these are my associates" Arthur whipped out his badge and flashed it in front of Frank's eyes as he introduced Pippa and Jack as well. Frank reached out to catch it, holding it in the air to make sure that it was genuine. Was Frank always this cautious, or was there a spate of people using fake badges?

"Has Gavin done anything wrong?" Frank asked.

"That's what we're trying to ascertain. Is there some place we could speak privately?"

Frank glanced around. Given the late night there was nobody else around.

"Whatever you have to say, you can say it hear."

Arthur kept his voice low anyway. "I'm afraid to inform you that I believe there has been a murder. We discovered that your employee, Jessica has died."

Frank blinked slowly, twice, then he frowned. He glanced toward Gavin. "And what has Gavin got to do with any of this?"

"That's what we were trying to figure out. He was near the scene of the crime as we were leaving," Arthur said.

"And where is this scene?" Frank asked. Pippa described the room to him. Frank's frown deepened. "That room is off limits to anyone but staff. What were you doing in there?" He loomed over Pippa, but Pippa was not going to allow him to intimidate her.

"I was trying to find Jessica because I wanted to know if we would be able to store the wedding cake here for a few days. She was overseeing the wedding reception that is going on as we speak."

"I know what she was doing," Frank spat. "But that doesn't give you the freedom to walk around my hotel as you like. The signs are there for a reason. Or perhaps suspicion should fall on you," he added, sneering this time.

"Pippa has my full trust. All we want is to try and get to the bottom of this. I'm sure you are quite disturbed that you have lost one of your employees. We must find out what has happened and how she died," Arthur said, trying to keep the peace.

"Indeed we must. We have to put a stop to the party right now. The murderer might be in that hall. I don't know why you're coming to me when you have at least a hundred suspects in there," Frank flung his arm in the general direction of the hall.

"We thought we would start with the staff first, considering they would have known her better," Arthur said, again straining to be polite in the face of such rudeness. Frank rolled his eyes.

"There's nothing wrong with my staff. We're a good team here. Everyone pulls together and we work well, isn't that right Gavin?" Gavin nodded sullenly, although Frank continued speaking without paying any attention to Gavin's words. "The only people we don't know about are the guests. It's far more likely that one of them is responsible. I am not going to have my staff discriminated against like this. I want to find out what happened to Jessica, and I want to find out now," he growled and pushed past Arthur toward the hall. It seemed as though Pippa was not going to get her wish and protect the sanctity of Tim and Callie's wedding day. They were going to have to cope with the grim shadow of murder hanging over them.

Frank burst through the door and marched to the DJ booth. He leaned into the DJ's ear and told him to cut the music, which stopped abruptly. Frank also gave a signal to Gavin, who turned the lights on. The hall was suddenly bathed in the bright luminescence of the electric lights and it dispelled some of the intimacy and magic caused by the reception. People blinked as their vision adjusted, and Pippa rushed to Callie's side. Her face was a picture of confusion.

"I'm so sorry about this Callie," Pippa whispered, but she was unable to give the full story before Frank's voice boomed through the microphone.

"Good evening guests. My name is Frank Hancock and I am the manager of the hotel. I do apologize for this

29

interruption in your evening, but I'm afraid that an urgent matter has arisen that requires me to bring this reception to an early end. It's a matter of security I'm afraid, and I really can't do anything else. I hope that your evening so far has been wonderful, and once again I am sorry for bringing the party to an end a few hours before you were ready. I will of course extend an invitation to the happy couple to come back here for a free meal and some other conciliatory matters that I shall talk to them about later, but for now I must ask you to return to your rooms and wait for further instructions. The police will be speaking to you in good time, and if you are not staying at the hotel then please leave your contact information. That is all," When Frank placed the microphone down and a heavy boom thundered through the hall. There was much confusion and people muttered and complained, annoyed that their good time was brought to an abrupt end.

"What's this about Pippa? What's happened?" Callie whispered.

"It's Jessica. She's been killed."

Callie gasped and a look of horror was upon her face. Frank was getting agitated because there were a great many people who weren't making any motion to move, instead preferring to complain and try and get the night back on track. Callie cleared her throat and clapped her hands, climbing onto a chair to get people's attention.

"I know that you all just want to keep dancing and keep having a good time, but I'm sure the manager wouldn't be asking us to do this if it wasn't a serious matter. Let's do what he and the police ask, and I'm sure that everything will work out well in the end. Let us reflect on how good the day has been already, and don't let this sour your mood. I know it's not going to make me unhappy!"

Callie's words mollified a lot of the unhappy people, and while they still grumbled they began to file away up to their rooms, following Frank's orders. Frank seemed to be relieved as well. Pippa squeezed Callie's hand in gratitude for being able to handle the situation, but now it was time to try and solve the case. She and Arthur walked back over to Frank, while Jack spoke with Callie and tried to explain to other people why they had to return to their rooms, without discussing the sensitive matter that someone had been killed.

"Would you be able to tell us a little more about Jessica?" Arthur asked.

Frank scowled. "I don't know why you want to speak to me so much. Go and ask them some questions. One of them must have seen something," he pointed to the guests who were milling around the hall.

"I understand you must be upset that one of your employees has died," Arthur said. He was interrupted by Frank. Anger blazed in the manager's eyes.

"Of course I'm upset," he hissed, keeping his voice low. "Jessica was an asset to this hotel. She was probably the hardest worker I had, and she was a good person. I don't know why anyone would want to kill her. Are you even sure this is murder? I know it's unthinkable, but what if she did just die naturally? Or, heaven forbid, what if she killed herself?"

"We think it's unlikely that she would have died of natural causes, but of course we can't rule out any possibility until the body has been examined. Do you think she would have had reason to kill herself?" Arthur asked.

"Oh I don't know," Frank waved a hand dismissively through the air. "She always seemed like she could handle pressure, but I suppose you never know what's going through someone's mind." He punctuated his words with a sigh.

"I should also remind you about Gavin. He said that he didn't mean to do anything, and was in quite an emotional state," Pippa said. Frank's eyes blazed once again. The slight glimpse of grief was overwhelmed by a raging fury, and this was accompanied by a harsh edge to his voice, so much so that it almost seemed his words were slashing through the air.

"There's no need to involve Gavin in this. You shouldn't harass innocent people. He's young and he's always had an anxious temperament. He lets things get to him and he was probably distressed by seeing three non-employees coming out of a staff room. I've tried to help him get better at confrontation, but he's still learning, and it's not going to help his confidence to be chased through the halls of this hotel."

"That may be so, but we still need to speak to him," Arthur said.

"And you can, but not until tomorrow. I am not going to have him questioned when he's in such a vulnerable state. I'm sure there must be laws about the welfare of people. Don't you have a duty of care to them?"

"You seem quite concerned about his wellbeing," Pippa pointed out. Frank gave her an icy glare.

"Of course I do. He's my employee. I care about all of them and I'll do everything I can to make sure they are protected. Unless you're going to arrest him I think it would be best if you question him after he's calmed down. He's not going to be in any fit state to answer questions if you go after him now. Besides, there are plenty of other people who you can talk to in the meantime."

Arthur and Pippa exchanged a wearied look. They certainly weren't going to arrest Gavin, and right now they needed to try and keep Frank calm because if he chose to he could make their lives difficult.

"Indeed there are, so you can't think of anyone that would have had a dispute with Jessica?" Arthur asked.

"Of course not, she had a good relationship with everyone. She was a hard worker, she helped out others when they were in need. She had a bright future ahead of her. One day she could have even managed a place like this herself." He lowered his voice and his gaze flicked around the room. "But if you ask me it could be one of the guests. You know what it's like at a wedding reception. People tend to get a bit rowdy, they start to get ideas. Jessica was always friendly with the guests. Maybe one of them took it a bit far and wanted more from her?"

"Do you have any evidence to support this?" Arthur asked.

Frank reared back and frowned. "Of course not."

"Then I suggest you leave the theorizing to us."

Pippa piped up with a question. "Is there any CCTV footage in that room?"

"No, unfortunately it's been malfunctioning for some time. I never thought to get it fixed because the staff didn't like being monitored while on their break," Frank sighed, wearing a look of lament.

"I suggest that you fix it as soon as possible to prevent something like this from happening again, even if it's not going to help Jessica," Arthur said. Frank nodded, and then excused himself by saying that he had to go and tell the rest of the staff, as well as make sure that nothing else untoward happened in the hotel. He would also need to sequester the room so that nobody entered and looked at the dead body. Arthur jerked his head to the side, indicating for Jack and Pippa to join him outside. The fresh air rolled in off the sea and brought a chill that made Pippa's teeth chatter.

"What did you pick up from other people Jack? Any of them seem guilty to you?" Arthur asked.

Jack shrugged. "Nothing jumped out at me. People are confused, naturally, and disappointed."

"I don't like Frank," Pippa said.

"Neither do I, but I have to commend his loyalty to his staff," Arthur replied.

"Isn't it quite convenient that there's no security footage?"

"Of course it is, but we don't know that it means he has anything to do with it. I have to say I don't like the way he's trying to figure out what happened. If anyone was upset that Jessica rebuffed their advances then I'd have to assume the murder would have been a violent, spontaneous one, not one that was calculated. Did any of the guests have any long interactions with Jessica?"

Pippa thought for a moment. "I don't think so. Only Tim, Callie, and myself. She was our point of contact with the hotel and she was always accommodating. We never had a problem with her, and as far as I'm aware she didn't have a problem with us either."

"Poison is a calculated weapon, one wielded by someone who knows what they're doing and has a specific target in mind. It's also one that suggests they want to remain hidden. While we can't rule out that it was one of the guests, I think it's likelier that the culprit is someone who works at the hotel."

"And the one who knows something is Gavin," Pippa added.

"And we've been warned off him."

Was that because he knew something, or was Frank genuine in his protective manner? There was most definitely something amiss at the hotel, and Pippa was determined to get to the bottom of it. It seemed, however, that they were going to have to wait until the following day before they could continue with the case, so Arthur told them to head back to the farm and rest.

The only one who was reluctant to leave the hotel was Jasper, who had created quite a connection with the other dog. Upon leaving, his head drooped and his tail barely wagged at all.

"Looks like someone was bitten by the love bug," Jack joked as he glanced into the rear view mirror.

"It's okay Jasper, we'll be heading back to the hotel tomorrow and I'm sure you can see your new friend again then," Pippa reassured her canine companion. Jasper's mood seemed to improve after this.

They returned to the farm. Pippa let her hair loose and took off her earrings, while Jack unbuttoned his jacket and draped it on the back of the chair. He boiled water in the kettle and made them a pot of tea.

"I feel so bad for Callie and Tim. I hate that their special day has been ruined like this," Pippa said.

"I suppose the day has been ruined, but they still have their whole lives together and that counts for something. I hope they're keeping that in mind. Besides, with the party ending early it just gives them more chance to be alone on their wedding day. I don't think they'll be complaining about that," Jack gave her a knowing wink. Pippa blushed.

"I don't know what to make of this case though. Everything was going so well, and then Frank is so demanding. Something tells me that Gavin knows something."

"I got that impression as well," Jack said. He handed a steaming cup of tea to Pippa, who took a sip, barely noticing how hot it was because her mind was whirring with various ideas and theories, running back what she had seen through the night in the hope that she might lock onto something that would shed light on the situation.

"So this is what our life is going to be like," Jack commented wryly, although Pippa was so distracted that she didn't quite catch the humor in his voice. She looked down into the dark tea.

"I know it's not normal, and I'm sorry for that, but I can't give it up. I can't turn my back on mysteries like these because Jessica might be dead, but that doesn't mean she doesn't deserve justice or help. I feel a calling toward them. It feels like God put me on earth to help people in this way."

Her tone was agitated, but Jack soothed it by reaching out and placing a warm hand upon hers. He smiled at her and she lifted her gaze to look at him. "I wasn't trying to be critical Pippa. I know how important this is to you, how important it is to everyone. I've known for a long time that this is who you are, and I admire you for it." He took a moment to compose himself before he spoke again, as his words were tinged with emotion. "I shut myself away from the world for a long time. I still saw people and I went out, but my life was one of routine. All the days blurred into each other and any communication I had with people was artificial. Gordon kept coming around under the pretense that Jasper had led him here, but I knew he was just checking up on me and making sure that I wasn't losing myself in my solitude. He was a good man." Pippa smiled at the memory of her grandfather. "And you're a good woman. You've shown me how great an effect someone can have on the world, and other people.

I'm a different man than I was when you arrived here Pippa, a better man. You've reminded me how good and rewarding it can be to be a part of the wider world, and I wouldn't want you to change at all. The only thing I'm worried about is your safety, but in that I have to trust God to watch over you."

She extended her other hand to meet his. Their fingers linked in with each other and their palms pressed against each other. She stared into his eyes, and when she did so it felt as though she was staring into the horizon, seeing both her future and their future combining into one. Her grandfather had saved Jack from solitude, and now he had saved her. They leaned over the table and their lips met in a gentle kiss. There had been a murder, but love had won out. If it was true for her and Jack then she was certain it would be the same for Callie and Tim. She and Jasper returned to their converted barn apartment, both of them equally lovelorn.

4

Jack decided to remain on the farm while Pippa returned to the hotel to investigate the case. As much as she would have liked to have Jack beside her, Pippa could not take him from his daily duties on the farm. There was much that depended on his efforts, and she did not wish to steal him away from his job. Besides, it wasn't as though she and Arthur could not handle things at the hotel. They had formed a good team before and would no doubt find their way to the truth again, or so she hoped.

When they reached the hotel, Jasper's ears pricked up and he began panting, no doubt anticipating a reunion with his new friend. Pippa smiled and thought it sweet. There were some people in the world who did not believe that animals were capable of emotion and that it was all mere projection from humans, but Pippa would dare them to spend time with a faithful companion and continue to make that argument in the face of such overwhelming evidence. She had felt Jasper's love and devotion in all the time they were together, and nothing would ever be able to convince her otherwise.

And was it this same kind of dogged devotion that drove Frank to protect his employees, or was there something more sinister going on? Pippa and Arthur both agreed that their first point of contact should be Gavin. He was the one who had been the first on the scene, he was the one who had run away, and Pippa couldn't shake the fact that he had said, 'I didn't mean to do anything.'

They asked around and eventually found that he was out on the golf course, collecting balls. He was not happy to see them. He tensed up as soon as they appeared and his eyes darted from side to side, as though he was looking for a way out like a trapped animal.

"Gavin, you remember me, I'm Constable Bell," Arthur said. Gavin nodded, although he kept his mouth clamped shut. "We're hoping to ask you a few questions. Are you feeling better after last night?" Gavin nodded again. "I first want to apologize for what happened. We were just trying to get information and did not mean to startle you or make you feel threatened. I hope that after a night to sleep on it you are able to recollect what happened last night?"

Gavin stared at them blankly.

"Gavin, anything you tell us, no matter how small, might help us to catch Jessica's killer. We're only trying to find out what happened to her. We're only trying to get to the truth. Is there anything you can tell us that might help shed some light on what happened?" Pippa asked, wearing a beseeching smile.

Gavin scratched the back of his neck and sniffed. "I don't have anything to say," he mumbled.

Pippa and Arthur glanced toward each other. "Gavin, you do realize that all we're trying to do is help. Now, last night you told us that, and I quote, 'you didn't do anything,' now what did you mean by that?"

"I didn't mean anything."

Arthur stifled a breath. "You must have meant something Gavin, or do you just go around saying things without meaning?"

Gavin wore a puzzled look and his tongue darted out, licking his lips. "I just... I thought you were going to accuse me of something. I wanted to make sure you knew that I hadn't done anything. You chased me after all."

"What would we accuse you of Gavin? Did you know that Jessica was dead?"

Pippa asked the pertinent question. If he did then it shed a lot of light on the case, for Pippa had been alone when she discovered the body. There had been a small window where Gavin might have entered the room as well, but if this was the case then she didn't understand why he wasn't simply coming out with the truth.

"I don't know. And no. I just... I don't know anything and I don't have anything to say. I need to get back to work," Gavin said, his words so blunt they punched the air. He walked away, and since they were not going to charge him with anything, Arthur and Pippa could do nothing about it. They sighed.

"That doesn't sound like the boy we spoke to last night," Arthur remarked.

"No, it certainly doesn't. In fact he's acting more like Frank. I wouldn't be surprised if Frank told him to say that."

"Which begs the question, what does Frank not want him to say?"

Without any firm evidence to go on it was difficult to cast aspersions around. If Gavin wasn't going to talk then Frank wasn't going to give them anything helpful either. During the night the coroner had come to collect the body, and Arthur and Pippa were sure that the autopsy would shed some light on what had happened. It might actually confirm their suspicions that Jessica had been poisoned, and if so might well identify the exact poison that was used. Until then they had to keep plugging away in the hope that someone would be able to tell them something useful.

Unfortunately, the guests at the hotel were mostly complaining about the fact that they could not leave. Now that the wedding was over they wanted to return to their normal lives, but instead they had to remain in the hotel. There were so many of them that Pippa and Arthur couldn't hope to question them all before the day was over, and the ones they did question didn't even know who Jessica was. She had done her job well and remained invisible to most of the guests. Jasper was proving to be less help than usual because he was preoccupied with finding the dog he had bonded with. He walked around the area where the dog had been sitting. Her scent must have lingered. Jasper whimpered and stared toward the door, as though he was waiting for this dog to appear.

The hall had not been entirely cleaned away. On one of the tables there was a spare disposable camera, and while Pippa stared at it she was suddenly struck by an idea. She snapped her fingers and told Arthur there was something else that might have captured some evidence; the pictures. People had been photographing each other all night, so perhaps something had been captured in a photo that could point them in the right direction. Maybe Jessica was speaking to someone, or maybe it even showed someone following her out of the room. Arthur thought it was a long shot, but he decided it was a lead worth investigating. They decided to come back to the hotel later, because if the pictures showed any evidence then they could use it to ask more informed questions or narrow down the people of interest.

Callie and Tim welcomed them in.

"I'm so sorry to disturb you, and I'm really sorry about what happened last night. It wasn't fair that your party was cut short," Pippa said.

Callie didn't seem to mind too much. "At the end of the day we are married, and now we have the rest of our lives to spend together. One night isn't going to ruin our marriage."

"And I'm just glad it wasn't anything to do with me!" Tim cried out. Pippa suppressed a smile. He had already been caught with two dead bodies. A third would have been most unusual, and most unwelcome.

She indulged Callie and Tim in a few brief words about the previous day, for of course the newlyweds wanted to revel in the warm memory of their wedding, despite the obvious shortcomings of the day. It was a time that would live long in their memories, but for now they were eager to stretch it to its limits. Pippa could tell that Arthur was becoming frustrated, for of course time was of the essence. Eventually Callie mentioned the disposable cameras and Pippa was able to use this to segue into what they were hoping to achieve. Callie said that the pictures were being developed as they spoke; Tim had dropped them off in the morning because they couldn't wait to see the kind of photos that had been taken. Pippa was delighted to hear this and got the details from the newlyweds. They were being developed at the local pharmacy, which had a dark room facility.

Callie and Tim were dragged around, as was Arthur. The person in charge of developing the photos said that it was going to take some time, but after some beseeching words from Callie, and some insistent words from Arthur, the developer agreed that he could move some things along and make sure that the pictures from the wedding became a priority. However, he told them, he could not make the pictures develop any faster because he could not control the chemicals. As such it was going to take a short while to get them back. Arthur said he would wait with Tim and Callie, and in the meantime Pippa decided that she was going to visit Braw Ben to discover what this surprise he had for her was.

Braw Ben smiled as Pippa entered, and he opened a bag of treats for Jasper, tossing one through the air. Jasper watched it intently and then leaped up, plucking it out of thin air. He gnawed on it as he settled beside his favorite place by the hearth. Braw Ben chuckled as he watched Jasper; the dog never failed to amuse him.

"That was an interesting night to say the least, so what happened at the hotel then?" Braw Ben asked.

"Unfortunately one of the hotel staff died, we think murdered," Pippa said. Braw Ben's face fell.

"I'm sorry to hear that. No wonder the party had to stop quickly."

"Indeed, I don't suppose you saw anything?"

Braw Ben shook his head. "Unfortunately I didn't. But then again I wasn't paying attention to anything other than the party. You could have had a gorilla walk through that place and I wouldn't have noticed," he chuckled.

Pippa offered him a polite smile. "I didn't just come here to talk about the party though. You mentioned that you had a surprise for me?"

Braw Ben snapped his fingers and seemed pleased that she had remembered. "Give me a minute," he said, and ventured toward the back, disappearing into the nether realm of the bar in which Pippa had never dared to tread. While this happened she was alone in the bar and she turned around, thinking about what this place must have been like in its heyday. It seemed that so many things were lost in the world, left behind in the past and were impossible to recapture, no matter how many people yearned for it. Her thoughts were interrupted as Braw Ben returned, clattering through a door that slammed of its own accord as he let it swing shut. Something sparkled in his hand, as he set it on the bar. It was a gold ring, perfectly round, with a studded diamond set into it. Pippa stared at it. It took a few moments, but then recognition twigged in her mind.

"Is that…?"

Braw Ben nodded. He beamed proudly. "It certainly is. That there is your grandmother's wedding ring."

"But how?" Pippa reached out and picked it up, tentatively at first, as though she was afraid that it was an illusion that would disappear upon her touch.

"Well, you see, around the time your dear grandmother died, I was courting a lass, Megan was her name, anyway, we were very close and I thought she was going to be the one who would… well," he cleared his throat and moved on swiftly from the subject. "Gordon told me that he had kept your grandmother's ring because she knew how valuable it was and she didn't want it to be wasted under six feet of dirt, never to see the light of day again. She wanted someone else to enjoy it, and when Gordon knew that I was going to ask the question, well, he gave it to me. Now, I was honored, obviously, but I thought it should stay in the family. He said that he only had a granddaughter left, and he didn't think she was the marry type, so he wanted to make sure it would go to someone who would make use of it." As he said this, Pippa winced and found herself filled with shame.

"Anyway, I ended up asking Megan, and although she was impressed with the ring, she wasn't impressed so much with the life I could offer her. She left and Gordon told me that I should keep a hold of it, just in case. Well the years passed and I started to forget about it, and then he died. It was only when I was doing some spring cleaning that I came across it again and I thought that you should have it. It was always intended for you Pippa. And given how you and Jack are looking, maybe it was just waiting for the right time. These things have a way of doing that, don't they? Anyway, you take it and you look after it. I'm sure your grandmother would have wanted you to have it," he said, patting her hand. Pippa held the ring tightly in her hand. It was just a piece of jewelry and should not have held so much significance, but it was a link to her past, to the people she had lost, and it was also a symbol of the undying devotion that her grandparents had shared. Tears filled her eyes and she was overwhelmed by emotion, reaching over the bar to grab Braw Ben in a tight hug. She knew he would never have known how much this would have meant to her, but she pocketed the ring and kept it close in her hand, feeling that she might indeed have a use for it soon. She resisted the temptation to test what it looked like on her finger though, not wishing to tempt fate.

Pippa rushed back to the pharmacy, although there was no urgency as they were still waiting for the photos to be developed. Thankfully it wasn't much longer, and they were handed to Tim and Callie in thick wallets. They immediately opened them to pore over them, handing them to Pippa and Arthur. They tried to make sense of the chronology of events, piecing together the night in the photos based on whether people were sitting or standing. In some of them they could see Jessica in the background. Unfortunately due to the amateur nature of the photographers a lot of pictures were fuzzy and unfocused.

However, at one point Callie held a picture in her hand and wore a puzzled look upon her face. "You didn't introduce me to these. Are they more cousins of yours?"

Tim peered at the picture as well. "I thought they were people from Burlybottom. I don't know them at all."

"But I don't know them either. And if we both don't know them then how can they be at our wedding?"

It was certainly suspicious, and if there were unwanted guests they must have been skilled to avoid being detected. Pippa supposed that it would have been easy to blend into the crowd as people were always preoccupied with other things, but were they the ones who killed Jessica? It was always possible that people who had a grudge against her had found out when she was working and infiltrated the wedding so they would have access to her, and it was likely that she would never have known. They had to speak to these men.

They returned to the hotel and managed to find the room in which these men were staying, as well as their names. They were Paul and Cameron. It was Paul who opened the door. The room opened to show two single beds, and a window where the curtains were drawn open. Paul was a thin man with thinning hair, and blue eyes. Cameron was huskier and shorter. His hair was long, and his beard was dark and thick. They both looked concerned. Paul clutched the door as though it was a shield, tensing after Arthur introduced himself.

"We were wondering if you could explain why you were at the wedding of two people who don't seem to know you," Arthur said, producing the photograph of them at the reception. There was no mistaking that it was indeed them, and they sighed with frustration, annoyed at being caught. Paul relaxed a little and glanced at Cameron.

"Look, we didn't mean anything by it, alright? We just noticed there was a wedding going on and thought we'd head in for some free food. There's plenty to go around."

"And do you make a habit of doing this?" Pippa asked.

"Nobody really minds. Loads of people get invited to weddings who don't want to go anyway. It's just an easy way to get a good meal, and sometimes to meet new people," Cameron joined Paul at the door. "I don't know why there's such a hullabaloo about it. Is this lockdown really necessary just to find us? I mean we would have owned up to it earlier if it wasn't being treated so seriously. Neither of us want to get in trouble."

"I don't think you're going to get in trouble for crashing the party. It's more the murder that we're concerned about," Pippa said. The words dropped like a bomb and the men looked shocked. Paul's face paled.

"Murder?" the word stammered out of him.

"One of the hotel staff was killed. Since you weren't supposed to be at wedding perhaps she discovered you?" Arthur suggested.

Cameron and Paul both shook their heads vehemently. "No way. We might crash a wedding now and then, but we're not killers," Paul looked agape. "To be honest we didn't even stay all night. As soon as the manager came in we were one of the first ones to leave because we thought it might be about us, but we were thinking about leaving anyway."

"Why?"

"Well, sometimes the longer you stay at a party the more chance there is of you being discovered, especially if people start realizing that you don't belong. We tried to stay out of sight as much as possible. The patio helped with that. Not many people went outside, on account of the chill blowing up from the sea."

"Until the argument anyway," Cameron added.

"What were you arguing about?" Pippa asked.

"Oh, we weren't arguing. We just heard one. Didn't hear what it was about mind you, just raised voices. I guess the wind was blowing in the wrong direction or something. Whoever they were, they were pretty mad," Paul said.

Arthur told them not to go anywhere, and warned them that from now on they should start only attending weddings they were invited to. Paul and Cameron looked like admonished schoolboys. Although they trespassed and intruded on the wedding, their explanation was plausible and Pippa did not think they were the killers. But perhaps this argument was a lead to follow.

She, Arthur, and Jasper walked through the hotel and back around to the patio area. There were large doors at the rear of the hall that led to this outside part, which looked over the golf course. The flags fluttered in the gentle breeze. Pippa shivered a little as she stepped outside. Burlybottom on Sea was a lovely, beautiful place, but it was only warm in the depths of summer. The patio was made up of wooden decking that stretched all around the hotel. As Pippa followed it around, she looked up the sheer side of the hotel, wondering if anyone other than Paul and Cameron might have heard the argument. But then, to her dismay, she saw that the patio area led to the manager's office. Pippa threw a glance to Arthur and then rapped her knuckles against the door.

Frank was not pleased to see them, to say the least.

"Have you found the killer yet?" he asked, folding his arms across his chest.

"Actually we're looking into some information we just found. There were reports of an argument out here in this patio area. Perhaps, given that your office is so close, you might have heard something? They might even have come from this office itself."

Frank gave them a steely glare. He was still standing in the doorway, blocking their entrance in. His head hung slightly and he ran his hand across his jaw. He sighed.

"I suppose it's time to make my confession. The fact of the matter is that I have been having an affair with Jessica over the past few months, but I decided to end it to work on my marriage. Unfortunately we were not able to keep it as secret as I had hoped, as Gavin saw us. I was afraid of the truth getting back to my wife. I love her and I wanted to have a chance to make up for my mistake. Jessica didn't agree. She wanted to fight for what we had. She wanted me to leave my wife. She said she was willing to do anything to make it work, but that was untenable to me. I had made my decision."

"So that's what you were fighting about?" Pippa asked, keeping her anger at the man in check. How could he be so cruel as to use Jessica for as long as he wanted and then simply decide that he had had enough? It didn't seem fair, and then he implied that Jessica was being unreasonable.

"We were fighting because I told her that she either needed to accept a transfer to another hotel or get another job. Temptation would be too much, and I didn't want to make the same mistake again."

"So she was being punished for your indiscretion?" Arthur asked.

Frank's eyes twitched. Pippa did not think he was used to being called out on his behavior. "She was not being punished," he replied through gritted teeth. "She could have been promoted. There are a number of nearby hotels in the chain, and a fresh start would have done her some good. As I said, she was a diligent worker. That's part of what attracted me to her in the first place. But she felt more strongly about things than I had anticipated. I thought she would understand that I would want to fix my marriage. Frankly I'm not sure if this is a murder at all. I think she might have killed herself to get back at me. There are plenty of toxic chemicals in the hotel and she could have taken any one of them."

"There weren't any bottles found near her," Pippa said.

"She could have drank them in another room and then gone into the staff room. I think it was a message for me. It was, after all, where we first indulged our feelings for each other. The lack of security cameras meant that it was quite convenient for us," Frank said, almost with pride. It certainly went to explain why Frank had not been in a rush to fix the security cameras. "I'm sorry for all of this. I should have told you last night, but I was in shock. I was afraid that the truth might come out and my marriage would be ruined."

Pippa thought that his marriage was ruined already by his unfaithfulness, and if he truly wanted to protect it then he should never have cheated on his wife in the first place, but she did not say this. Arthur thanked him for his time and they turned away.

"What do you think about that?" Arthur asked.

Pippa considered the matter for a moment. "I'm not sure why he would lie about it because it doesn't paint him in the best light, and it would explain why he didn't try to fix the security cameras. Unfortunately I don't have a better theory to offer. There isn't any evidence to suggest anything else, and whether I like it or not, his explanation does make sense. They would have been working in close quarters, probably spending late nights together. I just think it's unfair that she's the one who had to be punished despite him being the one who cheated on his wife."

"I agree. Sometimes the hand of justice takes longer to work than we would like, but I'm sure that won't be the last time a man like him does something he's not supposed to, and next time I'm sure he will be the one who suffers," Arthur said. Pippa certainly hoped that would be the case.

They went back into the hotel and sent around a message that the guests could leave. Some of them were in the hotel lounge, and gave up a great cheer. Others would be told via a message delivered by the staff. Jasper saw his friend in the corner of the room and went to say hello. They nuzzled each other and circled each other, but unfortunately their reunion was cut short as the owner got up to return to their room. He snapped his fingers and, after a moment's hesitation, the white dog followed. Jasper's head hung down. He whimpered as he returned to Pippa's heels.

"Better to have loved and lost eh Jasper," she said, petting him in a loving manner, promising him plenty of treats when they got home to help mend his broken heart.

5

Pippa returned to the farm and made good on her promise to Jasper. He was a little downcast, but seemed settled enough. Jack welcomed her with a hug and a kiss, and then she told him what had happened.

"Something still doesn't sit right with me though. Would Jessica really have killed herself because of this? If she was truly as hard working and determined as I thought then wouldn't she try to expose Frank?" she asked.

Jack shrugged. "I suppose you didn't know her well enough for that. People in love don't always act rationally."

"No, that's true. I suppose I'm just frustrated about how Frank can make a mockery of marriage as well. I don't know why he bothered getting married if he thought it was possible to cheat on his wife."

"I agree. I would only get married if I knew it was going to last forever."

"Me too. I guess that's why I never made that promise to Clive. Deep down I must have known that at some point it was going to come to an end." She angled her head away and felt guilt burn in her heart as she thought about Clive falling to his death. She had worked through her grief, but there were still moments when it struck her. But she was also preoccupied by the feeling of the ring in her pocket. She felt its outline through the material of her jacket and her breath caught in her throat. She glanced toward Jack. She was almost tempted to present it now, but she wasn't sure they had been together for long enough yet. The last thing she wanted to do was ruin what they had by pushing too hard, and was getting married even what she wanted? Would she be happy being a farmer's wife, waking up every day to Jack's smile and going to bed every night to the feeling of his kiss lingering upon her lips?

The more she thought about it the more the thoughts appealed to her, but she became flustered and didn't wish to speak about anything to do with marriage any longer. She quickly excused herself after they had eaten and went back to her own part of the house where she bathed and tried to ease away the tension of an unjust killing. Part of her was tempted to find Frank's wife and tell her everything that happened, but she didn't wish to meddle. That was something her old neighbors would have done. No, she had to trust that Arthur was right; Frank would probably make the same mistake again and eventually be caught. She only doubted that she would be there to enjoy the schadenfreude.

The following morning Pippa was getting ready to take Jasper on a long walk, which she hoped would cheer him up following the disappointing end to his brief romance. However, before she left a car pulled up, the tires grinding against the gravel. Arthur emerged looking ebullient, waving a piece of paper in the air. He rushed up to Pippa and showed her a note that had been left at the police station. It was from a mystery person, telling them to meet at Beggar's Stone. Pippa arched an eyebrow, wondering if this was about the case at the hotel, or something else.

"Perhaps Gavin is ready to talk to us," she muttered, although she doubted it.

Pippa joined Arthur in his car and they drove to a forested area. The stone was a small monument that was said to have been where beggars gathered on a trail in olden times, hoping that people would share their fortune. They had to walk away from the car and follow a trail down, which Pippa did not mind as it gave Jasper an opportunity to stretch his legs, and he liked the treat of being interested in some new surroundings. When they reached the stone Pippa saw the small notation stating that this was one of the oldest stones in Britain. It was smooth and black, almost oily, and she couldn't remember seeing anything else like it.

They waited for a while, and started to wonder if anyone was going to show up, or if this had been a hoax. Pippa stared at the stone. It was the kind of thing that could conjure the imagination, and she wondered what it had been like in years past. There were benches surrounding the stone. Pippa and Arthur waited on them, while Jasper nuzzled around the area, getting his nose into all the bushes and bramble. Pippa called out a warning to be careful of bees, not that Jasper paid any attention to her. But then, suddenly Jasper's ears pricked up as he sensed something. Pippa nudged Arthur's arm and they looked around. Approaching the stone was a slender figure with a shawl wrapped around her head, obscuring their appearance. From the gait Pippa assumed it was a woman, and wispy strands of dark hair confirmed this as she grew closer. The woman looked up from beyond the shawl and it took Pippa a moment to place her, but it was the receptionist from the hotel, Rosie. Pippa had seen her a few times when visiting the venue with Tim and Callie. She had not been manning the desk on the night of the reception though.

"Rosie?" Pippa gasped.

As soon as her name was spoken, Rosie dipped her head and looked around warily, as though there were people watching for her.

"Did you leave the note at the police station?" Arthur asked.

Rosie nodded, and when she spoke it was in a low voice. Thankfully the area was quiet so Pippa had no trouble hearing her. "I had to speak with you. I know what really happened to Jess," Rosie said.

"We were told that she and Frank were having an affair. Is there any truth to that?" Pippa asked.

Rosie's face transformed immediately. The concern of being overheard was abandoned as she threw her head back and laughed scornfully. "Frank wishes that were the case. She never would have done that. She hated him."

There was an edge to her words that attracted Pippa's attention, and all but confirmed that something had indeed been amiss. "Why?"

"Jess was a professional. She cared more about that hotel than any of us, including Frank. She was the manager in all but name because Frank couldn't be bothered with anything he found boring. But one day Jess found out that Frank had been using the hotel to smuggle in stolen goods and drugs. There would be strange delivery vans appearing in the dead of night, and irregularities in the accounts. Jess saw it all, and she told some of us. She said that she was going to take it to the police."

"So what happened?" Arthur asked.

"Frank happened," Rosie wore a nauseated expression. "He found her nosing in his office and then he confronted all of us. He said that if anyone spoke out then they would lose their jobs and that nobody would ever believe them because he was the manager and his word was final. He's a scary man when he wants to be, and he said that this was the only way to keep the hotel running. He said that it's not as popular as it used to be, and so if we wanted to keep our jobs then we were going to have to turn a blind eye to it, because as soon as head office found that there was something wrong they would shut us down. I didn't like it, but I have bills to pay. We all do. I was ashamed, but I couldn't take the risk that he was right. It's not like there are many other places hiring around here, and I have kids to feed. But Jess wasn't built like that. If you told her not to do something then she would make sure she did it. She was determined to get evidence against Frank to prove that he was a criminal."

"Why did Frank keep her employed if she was so much trouble?" Arthur asked.

Rosie shrugged. "To keep an eye on her I expect. The only leverage he had over her was the job, and if she was allowed to leave then he wouldn't have known where she was."

"And other people knew this? So they might have been concerned that Jessica's actions were going to lead to them losing their jobs. That means other members of staff have a motive to want her dead," Pippa said.

Rosie's eyes went wide. "Oh no, nobody else is capable of killing her. Everyone loved Jess. Like I said, she was practically the one in charge. She was the one who always sorted things out. Frank just knows how to work the people at head office. He always took credit for her ideas, and he never let any of us speak to them, so they have no idea what's really going on. He holds all the cards and we just rely on him for our jobs. That's the only thing he has on us."

"So do you think that this evidence Jessica was gathering exists?" Arthur asked.

Rosie nodded. "It has to. It's what put her onto things in the first place. But if it does then it's in Frank's office, and he doesn't let anyone in there, not even the cleaning staff."

"Could you get us in?" Pippa asked.

Rosie's eyes went wide with fear. She shook her head. "I've done enough by telling you this. If he found out," she paused and swallowed deeply. "I don't want to end up like Jess." She then seemed to think she had said enough and turned on her heels, rushing away as though she was being chased by banshees.

"Do you think you can get a search warrant?" Pippa asked.

"For that I'd need at least a written statement, and I don't think Rosie is going to be willing to go on record. We're going to have to find some other way in. I doubt Frank is going to invite us."

"No, and I've just been thinking that when we spoke to him yesterday he was standing right in the doorway of his office, preventing us from seeing in. There has to be something in there, although I'm surprised that he would keep records if they were incriminating."

"Perhaps he has to for the sake of whoever he is working with, and to keep the accounts straight with the hotel."

"How would that work anyway?"

"I imagine that he invents fake guests who are said to be staying in the hotel, and then whatever money he receives from smuggling he puts through as income from the guests, likely skimming some off the top for himself. Those at head office see a prospering hotel, which secures his job and the jobs of all the people who work there, and if he does have their ear then they're probably quite content. As long as they see money coming into their account they won't be particularly bothered. But at least Rosie shows she has something of a conscience. We just need to find someone else who does, or at least someone who might find the police scarier than Frank."

"I think I know what you're getting at. Should we speak to Gavin again?" Pippa asked. Arthur nodded, and there was no trace of delight on his face at all.

6

They returned to the hotel. They stayed in the car and looked out toward the golf course to confirm that Gavin was still there. They observed him wandering about with a huge bag, picking up stray golf balls. Pippa and Arthur walked in brazenly, not asking permission and not seeking out Frank. They assumed he would find out about their presence soon enough, and perhaps the fear of the investigation not being over would make him paranoid, and paranoid people make mistakes.

The golf course stretched out across the land like velvet. There were only a few people playing, and they frowned with annoyance toward the interlopers, especially at the sight of a dog on the course, for they were afraid that Jasper would ruin the impeccable lawns. Indeed, Jasper was tempted by the sight of the bunker, only seeing in his canine mind a small beach, and Pippa always allowed him to have fun on the beach. This time, however, Pippa whistled and called him to heel. Jasper whined. He was not having the best time of it.

They strode across the golf course and as soon as they came within eyesight of Gavin he froze again.

"I already told you I don't have anything to say to you. I have a job to do. There's lots of golf balls to collect and I can't stand around here all day." Gavin's words should have been commanding and stern, but because he lacked the confidence of maturity the tone of his voice was uneven and faltering. He was as much a victim of Frank's reign of terror as the others had been.

"Why, would Frank threaten to fire you again?" Pippa asked wryly, cocking an eyebrow and folding her arms. Gavin's mouth hung open and he stared forward, as if he were expecting words to come out, yet none did.

"We know what's been going on lad," Arthur said, this time in a kindly tone, although the look in his eyes made it clear that they were not going to let Gavin get away with covering up for Frank.

"What? How?" Gavin stammered, recoiling in fright.

"Tell us about Jessica," Pippa said. "Were you friends?"

Gavin nodded numbly. He looked as though he had been stunned. "She trained me. She was friends with everyone. We all liked her. She was always there whenever we needed her."

"And she needs you now Gavin. Whatever happened to her we know that it's not fair. She didn't want to die. She didn't deserve to die. I know you're scared, but think about how Jessica was there for you. You can help her now if you just talk to us," Pippa's words flew out of her mouth as though they had wings. She gave an impassioned plea, and her face was strained with hope.

"We can protect you lad," Arthur added, stepping closer to Gavin and reaching a hand out. "All you have to do is tell us the truth, and help us out."

"What… what do you want me to do?" Gavin asked after a few moments of silence. Pippa smiled, happy that his conscience had won out. They explained to him their plan. Gavin gulped and was clearly scared. "You promise that nothing bad will happen to me?" He may have only been a year or so away from being legally considered an adult, but all Pippa saw when she looked at him was a child. Arthur reassured him that nothing bad would happen. All they needed to do was get into Frank's office.

Pippa and Arthur returned to the car with Jasper while Gavin went into the hotel. They needed to wait for an opportune moment to enter the office. Unfortunately, Frank had chosen this night to work late. While they were waiting, Pippa took the opportunity to speak with Arthur.

"Arthur, can I ask you a personal question? How did you know that Sophie was the one you wanted to spend your life with?"

Arthur's eyes twinkled. There were few things he preferred talking about than his great love for his wife. "It was early on when we were courting. I had bought her tickets to the theatre. There was a show that she wanted to see, but at the same time there was a crime spree in town and it was all hands on deck. I tried to beg for the time off because I knew how important it was to her, but duty called. I thought that would be the end of it. She was disappointed, of course, but she accepted that it was a part of the job. She said that the play would always come back around again, and all she hoped was that I was safe. We rearranged to see each other again, and I knew that she would not resent me for the job I had. It's all too common for police officers to marry people who end up becoming bitter about the job. The thing is it's never going to change. As much as I hate to admit it, crime is one of the few constants in the world, and we have to be vigilant to lessen its impact as much as possible. It's always going to be the same, no matter how long we are on the job for, so when you find someone who will stand by you and support you rather than resent the job for taking you away from them... well... it's priceless."

Pippa thought about what Jack had said and how he had claimed he was only concerned with her safety, and she smiled.

"Is there a certain farmer who has asked you to marry him?" Arthur asked.

Pippa chuckled. "Not yet." She fingered the ring in her pocket, and her mind turned to all the possibilities of the future…

Time passed. Gavin kept coming out and shaking his head. Arthur and Pippa were beginning to get frustrated. They got out of the car and approached Gavin.

"Is he still in there?" Arthur asked.

"He's not budging. I've been checking constantly. He must be busy," Gavin replied.

"Or he's scared about someone finding what he's hiding in there," Pippa muttered under her breath.

"Okay lad, here's what we're going to do. Try and lure him out. Say that there's been a spillage or something. While you're occupied with him we'll go into his office and see what we can find." Arthur suggested. Gavin's face turned pale at the sound of this, but he nodded anyway. Arthur and Pippa followed him into the hotel, but they stayed out of sight while Gavin approached the manager's office. He rapped his knuckles against the door.

"What is it?" Frank asked brashly.

"S-sorry to disturb you F-Frank, but I need your help," Gavin asked. The poor boy sounded as though he was a tower of teetering sticks that was about to topple over.

"There's an... um... a spillage!" Gavin said. Pippa cringed. He couldn't have sounded more uncertain if he tried, and it surely wouldn't have deceived someone as perceptive as Frank. Indeed, Pippa's heart sank as she heard Frank's reply.

"You don't sound too sure of that Gavin. They've gotten to you somehow, haven't they? I told you what was going to happen if you turned on me. It's not just your job on the line anymore boy. You should have known better. You should have trusted me!" he roared, and then Pippa heard a sharp thump and then a cry. She peered around the corner. The door burst open and the two men appeared on the patio. Frank looked like a giant compared to Gavin. His face was a picture of rage and he swiped at Gavin again with a hard fist. Gavin was just about to evade the blow and scampered back, almost losing his footing as he twisted and pushed through another door, this one labeled 'pool'.

Arthur, Pippa, and Jasper leaped into action. If Gavin got hurt it was their responsibility, and Pippa didn't want this on her conscience. There was no doubt in her mind that Frank had killed once, and he might be willing to do so again if he thought his secret was in jeopardy. Their footsteps clattered across the decking. Jasper reached the door first, but he had to wait for Pippa to catch up to him before it was opened.

As soon as it was, they darted in. The scent of chlorine filled the air, choking their nostrils, while the icy blue water stretched out in the long pool. A jacuzzi bubbled in the distance, but Pippa only had eyes for the fight that was unfolding in front of her. Both men had fallen into the water and were thrashing around. Great ripples spread away from them, almost becoming waves. It was difficult to see who was winning, but she heard muffled cries from Gavin as he begged for mercy. These cries were suffocated by the water as Frank loomed over him.

"Get away from him! Let him go now!" Pippa cried out. Jasper stood on the edge of the pool, reluctant to get in. Water was something he had never been fond of, and Pippa worried that the advantage of his agility would be negated in the water and make him vulnerable to Frank's strength. If he was capable of murder, then he was capable of hurting a dog.

Frank was distracted by her words and looked up. This brief interlude was enough to allow Gavin to twist away from his grip. The young man surged underneath the water, while Frank's hand reached down to try and grasp his leg. He ended up grabbing nothing but empty air. Gavin reached the side and pulled himself up frantically, rolling away from the pool, leaving a trail of water as he did so. He was panting heavily and his clothes were soaked through. Frank wasn't too far behind him, but Arthur, Pippa, and Jasper had already set off to cut him off. He waded through the pool and put his strong fingers onto the edge of the pool, but before he could climb out he was met with Jasper's low growl. The dog bared his teeth, making it clear to Frank that nothing awaited him but doom.

"It's time to come clean Frank. We have you dead to rights," Pippa said.

"You don't have anything," he said through gritted teeth, glaring at Gavin. He was soaked through too, but he was so filled with rage that Pippa could almost see steam rising from the water around him. Gavin had pulled himself to his feet and staggered back, eager to put as much distance between him and Frank as possible.

"We'll see about that. I think it's time I take a look in that office, if you'd be so kind as to guard the prisoner," she said to Arthur, and then gave a command to Jasper to stay and watch Frank. Frank's face twisted into a scowl and he looked from side to side for a way to escape, like a caged animal. But he was helpless.

Pippa's heart beat rapidly as she strode through the hotel toward the manager's office, hoping against hope that she would find what she was looking for. Frank had had plenty of opportunity to scrub his office clean of any evidence, and if so then he would remain a free man even if Gavin and Rosie testified against him. Justice for Jessica hinged on her being able to wade through his office and find what little treasure there was.

She had found treasure once before though, so she was confident she could do it again.

The office was a decent sized room with a door that led onto the patio. There was another door that led to a hallway inside the hotel. There was a glass pane in each of these doors, although blinds had been drawn over these, as well as over the window. An electric light hummed instead, casting a dim glow over the room. A desk sat in the middle of the room beside the window. Filing cabinets dotted the walls. Pippa flicked through them and then went to the desk. She looked through the computer, but there was nothing there. She worked quickly, feeling the pressure of time upon her shoulders, thinking about Jessica with vomit on her face, Gavin cowering in the corner, Rosie hiding her face even when she was alone. There was a culture of fear that had been allowed to fester under Frank's watch, and it needed to end.

But where would he hide something?

After a fruitless search she leaned back in the chair and looked around. Would he be so obvious as to leave something in plain sight? She rifled through his drawers and cast her gaze all around the room, again and again in case she missed something. There were personnel files and rotas and documents from head office, but nothing that pointed to any criminal activity. Pippa was beginning to fear that they were completely wrong. After all, they only had Rosie's word to go on, but then her eyes caught a vent near the window. Perhaps… just perhaps…

She had to stand on the chair to reach it. She felt around the hatch. There was a crisscross pattern of metal, so it was difficult to see behind it, but when she tried to pry it away it came loose. It should have been screwed tightly to the wall. Feeling a rush of adrenaline, she struggled with all her strength to peel this hatch off the wall. The metal dug into her fingers and pain ran up her arm like a spike as she grit her teeth and pulled. She almost lost her balance as she strained so hard, but then the vent cover came away and she was left gazing into an abyss, but this abyss was not empty.

She reached in and pulled out a sleek silver laptop. She opened it on the desk, but it was password protected, so she took it back to the swimming pool where the others were waiting for her.

"What's the password Frank?" Pippa asked.

"I'm not telling you," he replied curtly. "It's private property."

"You'll tell her, or I'll make you sit in a cell in those wet clothes all night long. You know the game is up Frank, it's just a matter of how long it takes us to untangle the threads you've woven. If you don't cooperate with us now then you could add a good five years to your sentence, at least."

Frank sighed and seemed to weigh his options. "Alright, but can I at least get out of the swimming pool?" he said.

"Password first," Arthur insisted. Frank rolled his eyes, but provided Pippa with a string of letters and numbers. She typed them in and the laptop opened to reveal documents detailing illegal transactions, both the goods that had been smuggled and who had been involved. Frank had pulled himself out of the water and was wringing out his wet clothes. Jasper was still on guard, while Gavin had moved so that Pippa, Arthur, and Jasper were between him and Frank.

"It's all here. Looks like you've been a busy man Frank, although I'm surprised that you kept such detailed records. Surely you knew that this would just make you look guiltier?"

"I thought it was a good insurance policy in case any of my... associates decided to try and turn against me. And I'm sure the police are going to enjoy knowing everything I can tell them about this smuggling operation. I hear they're quite open to making deals," Frank wore a smug smile on his face. Even when he lost there was a sense that he was winning somehow, and Pippa felt sick.

"That's not going to happen this time. You murdered someone," she spat.

"Did I? I don't believe there's any evidence pointing to that. I'm afraid to say that Jessica was distressed and probably overworked. I do regret that she died, but it seems like it's going to be a mystery."

"No it's not." Gavin spoke loud and clear, as though he had just found his confidence. The sneer fell from Frank's face and instead he glared at Gavin.

"Think carefully about this boy. I'm going to get out of this and if you turn against me I'm going to make life very difficult for you," Frank spat.

"You're not a king Frank. The only authority you have is in this hotel, and that's going to be stripped away from you as soon as you get arrested. Gavin, you don't have anything to fear from him any longer," Pippa said, hoping to galvanize Gavin so that he would not wilt in the face of Frank's domineering attitude. Gavin steadied himself and clutched his hands into fists.

"I saw him pour something into Jessica's drink while she was in the reception hall. He got it from the cleaning supplies. I didn't know what was happening at first. I didn't understand, but then I saw Jessica clutching her stomach and staggering to the staff room. Then you told me she was dead and… and it all makes sense."

"Could you identify which bottle he poured into Jessica's drink?" Arthur asked.

Gavin nodded, and that was all they needed to make an arrest. Arthur whipped out a pair of handcuffs and approached Frank. Pippa held her breath, worried that Frank was going to resist, but he just muttered and cursed under his breath as Arthur read him his rights. Pippa shut the laptop and held it firmly under her arm as she turned to Gavin.

"Thanks for your help Gavin," she said, although that seemed to prove small comfort to him. He wore a look of misery and spoke soft words.

"She needed my help and I kept quiet. I should never have let this happen. I should have stopped him when I saw what he was doing."

While Pippa agreed, she couldn't help but feel pity for the young man. There was still so much he had to learn about life, and it wasn't always easy to stand up to people when there were other factors to take into account, like a fearsome boss who wielded their power like a potent weapon. She was sure that Gavin would learn from this mistake and become a better person because of it. She turned to him and wore a sympathetic look.

"Gavin, what really matters is that you did the right thing in the end. Because of you the bad people that Frank worked with are going to be arrested and no matter what he thinks, he isn't going to get away from this unpunished. Jessica is in heaven right now and she's safe in the knowledge that justice will be served. Just make sure you keep thinking about that. You have a long life ahead of you and this isn't the only chance you're going to have to prove yourself. Believe me, I've learned that life is a learning process. We keep growing and we keep moving forward, and hopefully we keep improving. You're going to be alright. Keep your head up, stick to what you believe in, and trust in the people around you. Don't let Frank get in your head because the only thing he cares about is himself."

Gavin nodded. Pippa expected that he would take some time to heed her words, but she hoped that his life would not be ruined because of this. She dusted her hands as she watched Arthur leading Frank away. Pippa smiled toward Rosie as she left the hotel. Rosie looked away quickly, but Pippa knew that things would be better from here on out. With the information in the laptop the smuggling ring would be disbanded, and the hotel could get back to focusing on what it had been built for. Hopefully the next manager would not be the same kind of tyrant as Frank.

7

Pippa returned to the farm house, rubbing her eyes. Jack was there, waiting for her with a cup of tea. Jasper came in behind her, his feet padding against the floor. His bowl was filled with some sticky chunks of food. He began devouring it quickly and seemed happy enough. Pippa envied how easily he was able to move on from his fleeting romance. If only human emotions could be so uncomplicated.

She settled on the couch in the lounge and leaned her head back, massaging a knotted muscle in her shoulder. She described the case to Jack, who murmured along.

"At least you got your man in the end," he said.

"Yeah," Pippa sighed, "although I do think Jessica's death could have been avoided. I suppose it was hubris of Frank to think that he could have gotten away with it."

"He'd been getting away with so much else that he probably thought he was untouchable. I've known men like him before. They think they have the world on a string. I'm glad you were able to cut those strings away."

"It was quite funny to see him in the pool, all drenched and soaking," Pippa enjoyed some mild amusement. "But I certainly didn't imagine the wedding would end up like this."

"No, me neither, but then I suppose we can never anticipate what's going to happen. Were Tim and Callie upset about the way things turned out?"

"I don't think so. The ceremony was more important to them than the party, and they still had a good evening. We had all the important parts anyway. The other casualty was the cake. In all the confusion we never did get it stored, so that it had to be thrown away. The last time I saw them they were looking through all the pictures that had been taken. I think they're planning to display them in the community hall so that everyone can look at them, before they're all put into albums."

"That's a lovely idea," Jack's face warmed with the soft glow of happiness. "It really does make me feel good to know how the community is so tied together here. We're all one big family, for better or worse."

"But mostly for better," Pippa replied, smiling widely.

"I agree. Although I'm not sure I'm going to want to see pictures of me on display. I've never been the most photogenic. I bet they've captured me in the middle of eating something or doing something else embarrassing."

"Actually there are some rather lovely ones of you," Pippa said. She had tried to not let her attention wander too much when she had been poring through the photos before, but she had been touched by some of the pictures of Jack. "In fact there's one of us dancing that is really beautiful. The light catches us in such a way as to make it look like we're in a star."

"Well I suppose I shall have to look at these pictures then. Perhaps Tim and Callie will let us have a copy. It would be nice to frame it and hang it somewhere."

Pippa's eyebrows arched. It was the first time he had mentioned having a permanent reminder of them in his home. "You really think so?"

"Of course I do," he said, giving her a look that suggested he didn't know why she would ever think he wouldn't. Pippa reached down and massaged the ring that Braw Ben had given her. A lump appeared in her throat and her chest tightened. She kept telling herself that she shouldn't be this frightened, and yet she couldn't stop herself.

"Jack, I've been doing a lot of thinking lately," she began.

"Oh dear," he replied with a teasing smile. With one look

she was able to communicate that this wasn't a laughing matter. He remained silent as she continued.

"I've just been reflecting on my time in Burlybottom on Sea. When I look back at the woman who arrived here I'm not sure I recognize myself. I've changed in so many ways, and most definitely for the better. I think when I lived in London it was like I wore a costume of what I thought life should be like, or the woman I should be. But since returning here I've rediscovered what it is to be Pippa, and I think I needed that time alone. But I'm not sure I want to be alone anymore."

"Well that's good," Jack said.

"I mean, I know my life is not the most usual. I don't expect that I shall ever stop helping solve these mysteries now and then because I feel a calling toward it. I know that sometimes this puts me in danger and the last thing I want to do is to make you feel uneasy about anything."

"Pippa, you know I've already said that I'm not going to stop you from doing what you do best."

"I know, but I need to be frank about this with you Jack because it's important. I know how hard it was for you to move on from Emily. I don't want you to have to do that a second time."

"Are you saying that you want this to end because you want to protect me?"

Panic flared in Pippa's heart. "No, of course not," she spoke quickly. "I just want to make sure you know what you're getting yourself in for."

Jack smirked, as though he was going to give one of his quick witted answers, but the smile flickered away from his face, as though he thought better of it. He adjusted his position and clasped both of Pippa's hands in his. His tone was earnest.

"Pippa, you're right. It did take me a long time to move on from Emily. But losing her also gave me a reason to appreciate everything that comes toward me in life. When we first met I knew that you were different, I just didn't know how different you would be, or how strongly I would feel about you. There were times when I thought this part of me was dead, but you helped prove me wrong. I know that by accepting these feelings I am opening myself up to losing you, and if that does ever happen then it's going to be the worst pain imaginable. I think maybe that's why I was so quick to come to Leeds. I hate the thought of you being in danger, but that isn't going to stop me from loving you. Loving people always comes with a risk and I know from personal experience that even if you live a safe life you might still be in danger of dying. People can be taken from your life at any moment, so all you can do is appreciate them while they are here and try to make the best of the moments you do have. And I want to do that with you Pippa. I want to make the best of our lives."

A smile twitched on Pippa's face. "I'm glad you said that Jack because, well..." she then proceeded to take the ring from her pocket and held it in between the two of them.

"That's beautiful," Jack gasped. "Where did you get it from?"

"Braw Ben gave it to me."

"Oh really, I didn't know he felt that way about you," Jack quipped. He chuckled at his own joke, while Pippa gave him a look.

"This was my grandmother's ring. Apparently Grandad gave it to Braw Ben when Braw Ben asked his girlfriend to marry him. But she said no and left." Jack gave a quiet nod. "Grandad told him to keep it. He has done so until now, and he gave it to me, thinking that I should keep it in the family. I hadn't really thought about getting married, at least not seriously, but when he gave me this ring I just... I became overwhelmed and I started thinking about the way I want the rest of my life to play out. I used to judge my success in nothing but pure numbers, thinking that if I prospered financially then nothing else mattered. But I know that's not true now. When I think of the future I want to wake up feeling that I am a part of a family. I want to feel like I am growing with someone and I think... I *know* that I want that person to be you."

"Why Pippa Finn, are you asking me to marry you?" Jack asked with a cocked eyebrow.

Pippa glanced down at the ring and then back at him. She blushed. "I suppose I am. I hope that doesn't ruin the tradition."

"Well, you have never been a traditional woman Pippa," Jack replied with a warm smile. "And if that is what you're asking, then my answer would be yes, as I would hope your answer would be if I posed the same question."

"Of course it would," Pippa said. For a moment she sat there, stunned, for it had not really sunk in. It was only when Jack took the ring from her and placed it upon her finger that she realized she had just made a promise that would last the rest of her life, and there were no doubts at all in her mind. She had as much faith in him and the love they shared as she did in the Lord Himself. She and Jack shared an affectionate kiss as they sealed their promise to each other, and then she let out a delightful cry.

Jasper seemed to sense that something new and unusual was happening. He came running in from the kitchen and jumped on her lap. The three of them celebrated this news, and Pippa was reminded that while there were always grim things in the world, there were always joyful things to go hand in hand with them.

THANK YOU FOR CHOOSING A PUREREAD BOOK!

We hope you enjoyed the story, and as a way to thank you for choosing PureRead we'd like to send you this free Special Edition Cozy, and other fun reader rewards...

Click Here to download your free Cozy Mystery
PureRead.com/cozy

Thanks again for reading.
See you soon!

OTHER BOOKS IN THIS SERIES

Read them all...

If you loved this story why not continue straight away with other books in the series?

Inheriting A Mystery

The Secrets of the Sea

Mystery on the Doorstep

Hammer Home A Mystery

Three Salty Secrets

Death on Aisle Five

Dead & Breakfast

Family Secrets & Canine Conundrums

The Case of the Disappearing Fiancé

OUR GIFT TO YOU

AS A WAY TO SAY THANK YOU WE WOULD LOVE TO SEND YOU THIS SPECIAL EDITION COZY MYSTERY FREE OF CHARGE.

Our Reader List is 100% FREE

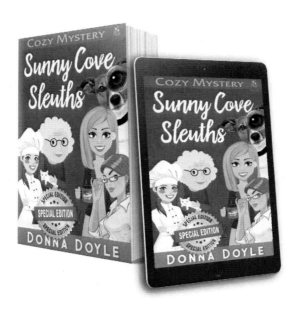

Click Here to download your free Cozy Mystery
PureRead.com/cozy

At PureRead we publish books you can trust. Great tales without smut or swearing, but with all of the mystery and romance you expect from a great story.

Be the first to know when we release new books, take part in our fun competitions, and get surprise free books in your inbox by signing up to our Reader list.

As a thank you you'll receive this exclusive Special Edition Cozy available only to our subscribers...

Click Here to download your free Cozy Mystery
PureRead.com/cozy

Thanks again for reading.
See you soon!